ERIC
AND THE MAD INVENTOR

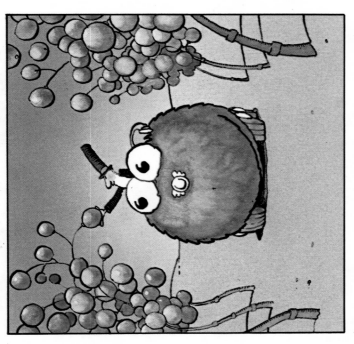

Pictures by
Malcolm Livingstone

Story by John Sheridan

Dedicated to our Dad

Published by Marshall Cavendish
Children's Books Limited,
58 Old Compton Street,
London W1V 5PA

Eric was a wild car.
He lived with his friend Mr Flywheel,
who was an inventor.

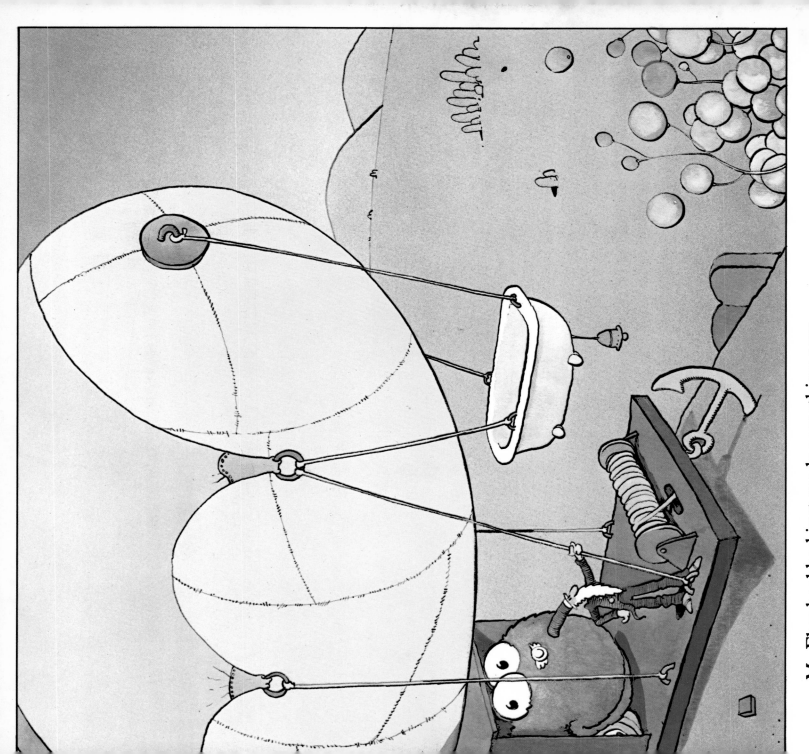

Mr Flywheel had just made something new.
It was a big balloon tied to a platform.
He filled it with floating pods.

When it was finished, they went up in the balloon. Up, over nearby towns they climbed. Soon, they were as high as the clouds.

The wind blew them gently out to sea. Eric and Mr Flywheel watched the sun set and then went to sleep.

Eric woke at dawn. "Where are we?" he thought. He looked down and saw something dark on top of the water far below.

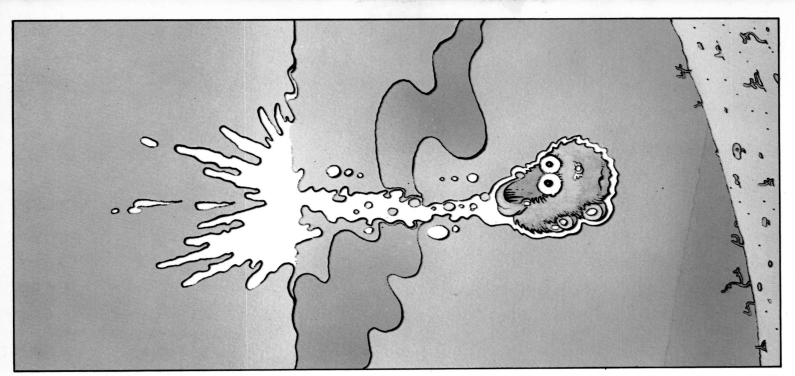

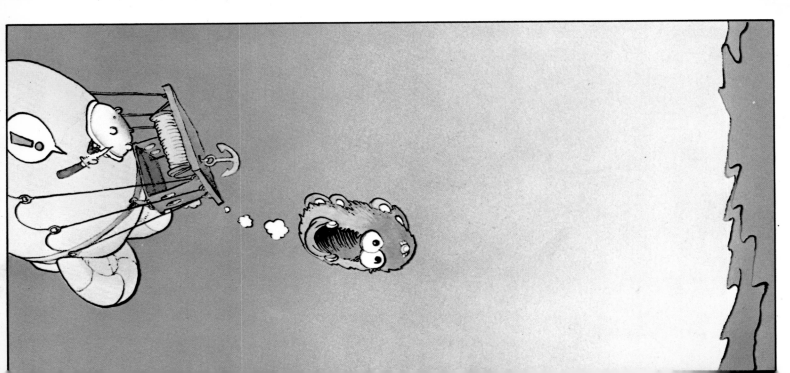

Eric leaned over the edge of the platform for a better look. He was so heavy that it tipped over. Eric fell into the sea!

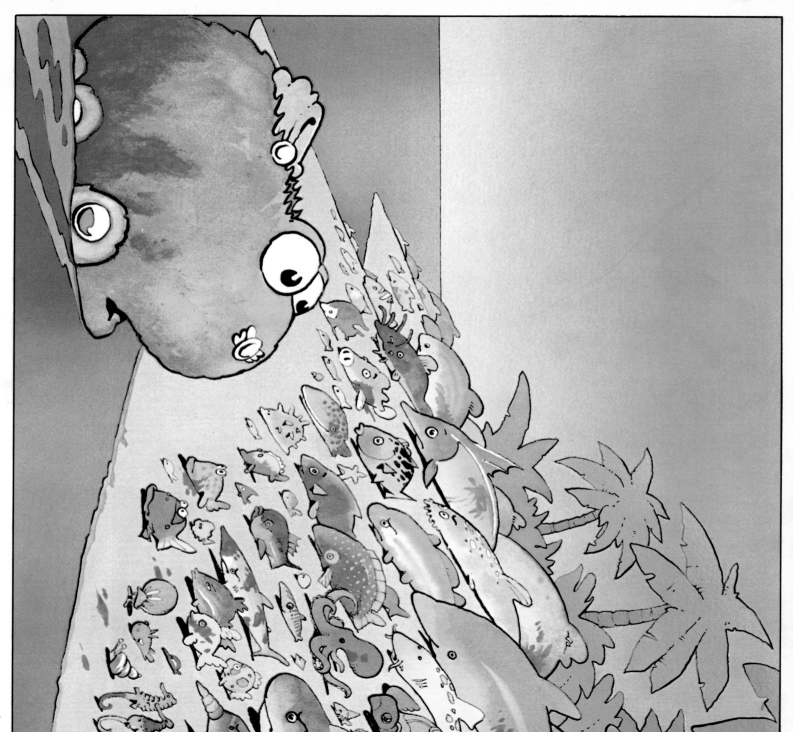

Eric came up near an island. There were a lot of fish on the beach. He saw that the dark stuff on him and on the water was oil.

"What happened?" he asked.
"We couldn't live in the sea anymore,"
said the fish. "There is more oil every day."

Mr Flywheel came down to find Eric.
Eric told him about the oil.
"We'll help the fish," said Mr Flywheel.

Mr Flywheel washed and Eric licked until
the fish were clean. Mr Flywheel said,
"Now let's find out where the oil comes from."

An octopus told them he had seen oil pouring from two pipes in the water. Eric and Mr Flywheel set off the way he pointed.

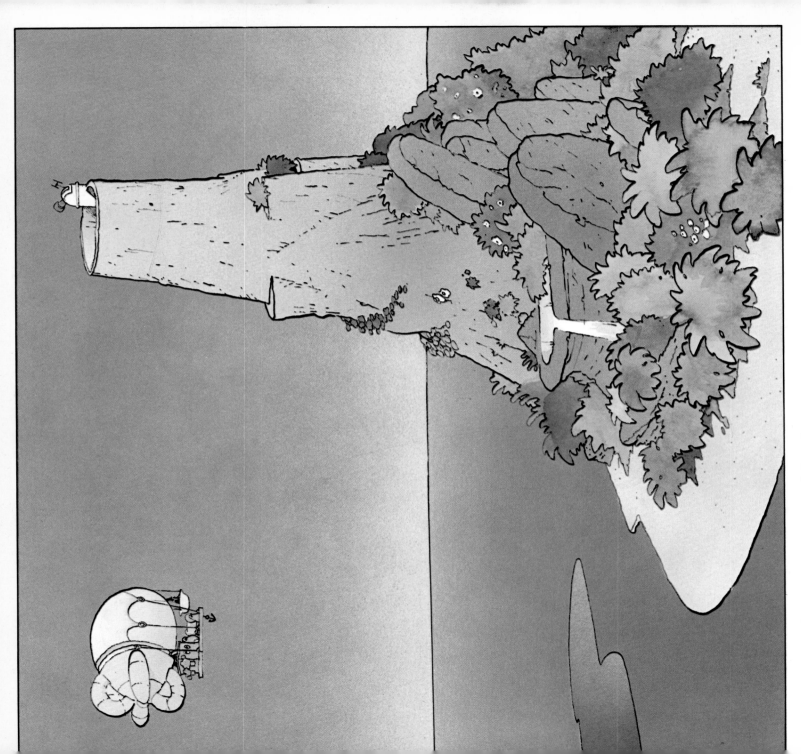

Soon, they were over an island.
"There's a volcano," said Mr Flywheel.
"Let's go down and see if anyone is at home."

As they came in to land,
a little man in a white coat looked up.
"Hello!" called Mr Flywheel.

"I am Mr Flywheel," he said,
"and this is my friend Eric."
"I am Dr Belfry. What can I do for you?"

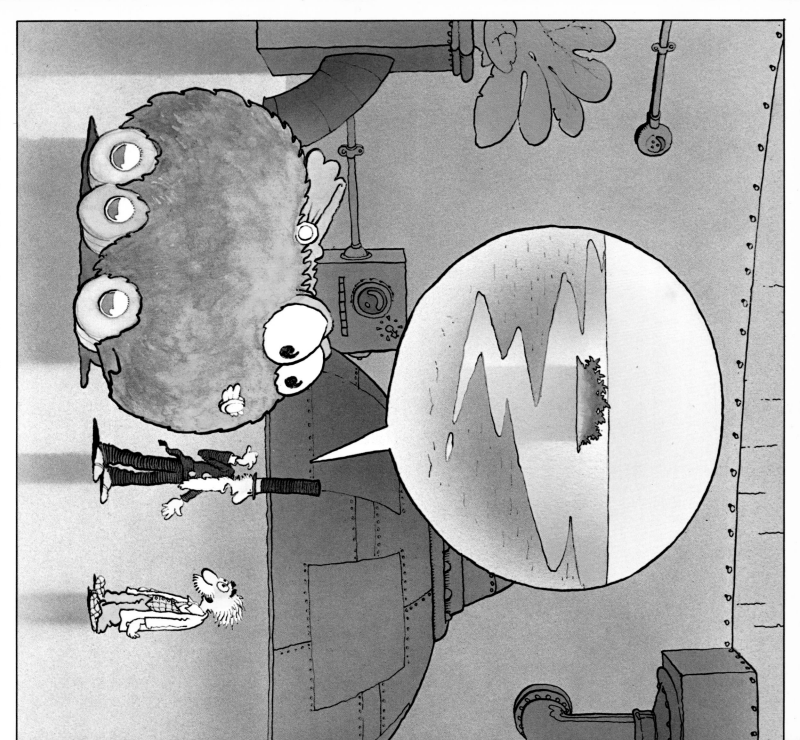

Mr Flywheel told him about the oil. "I don't understand. Where can it be coming from?" cried Dr Belfry.

He ran to one of his machines.
"Oh, dear. The oil is leaking from
the room where I grow giant peas!" he cried.

Dr Belfry led Eric and Mr Flywheel down to the main plant room. "Here we are," he said.

When Dr Belfry opened the doors, oil poured out. Dr Belfry exclaimed, "It's much worse than I thought!"

"The giant pea pods are so heavy that they have broken the pipes," Dr Belfry said.
"We must stop the oil," said Mr Flywheel.

Mr Flywheel turned off the tap on the pipe.
Dr Belfry cut down the pea pods.
"Now we must clear up the oil," he said.

Mr Flywheel could see giant plants everywhere. While they cleaned the room, Dr Belfry explained how he grew them.

"All this work has made me hungry,"
said Dr Belfry. "Let's eat."
Mr Flywheel could almost taste what was coming.

"I'm sorry, there's only bread and cheese," said Dr Belfry. "The giant plants look nice, but they taste awful."

Mr Flywheel was very disappointed.
While they ate, they worked out a plan
to help clean up the oil from the water.

The three of them worked all night to make a giant pump and then tied it to the balloon. Mr Flywheel set out to see if it worked.

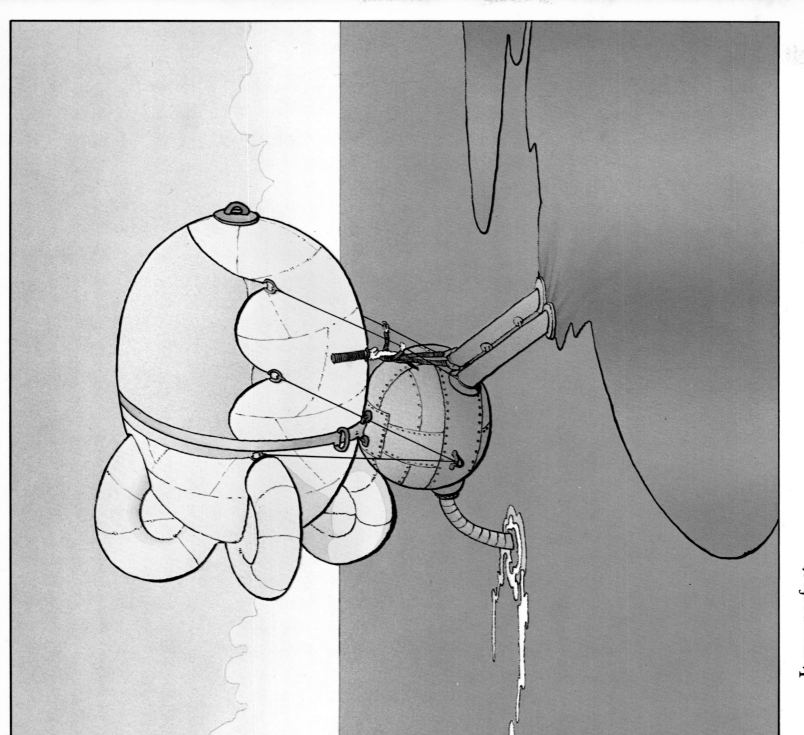

It was perfect.
The pump sucked up the oil and carried it back to a tank on the island.

The fish were very happy when they saw Mr Flywheel with the pump, cleaning up the oil on the sea.

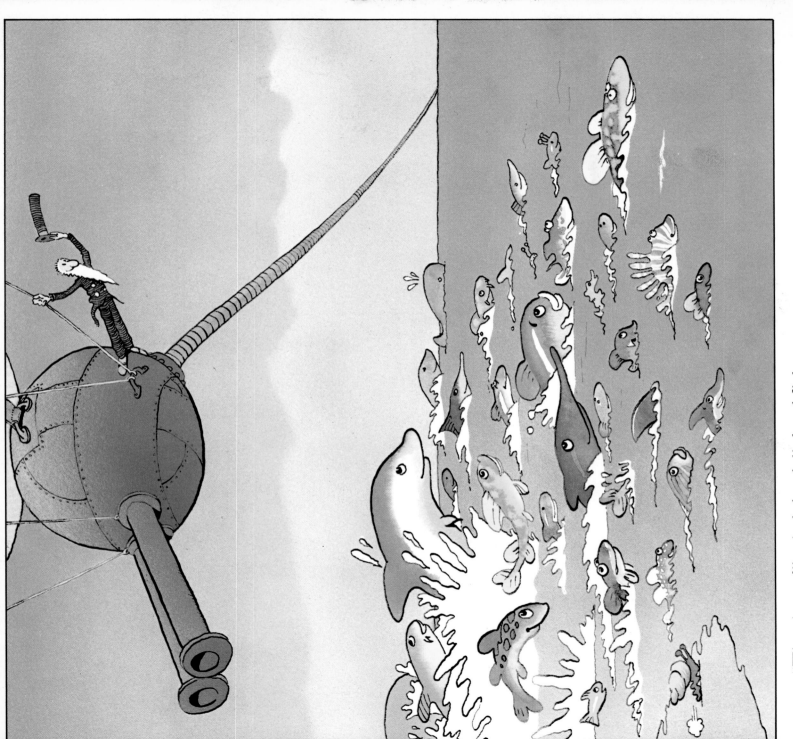

"Thank you!" cried the delighted fish.
They jumped back into the water and
Mr Flywheel returned to Eric and Dr Belfry.

Back on the island, Mr Flywheel brought out his food basket. "The cakes and fruit are small, but they all taste good," he said.

Later, they all went up in the balloon.
"There's really no use for my plants," Dr Belfry
said. "I forgot how perfect nature is already."

"Thank you for everything.
I will work on something really useful now,"
said Dr Belfry as he waved good-bye.